To the
Holly family
Enjoy all the
world's animals!

Jane K. Webb

FURRY FRIENDS

By

Jane K. Webb

Illustrated By

Micheline Grenier

First edition 2003
Second edition 2006
Third edition published in full color September 2013

JKW Press
PO Box 8177
Longboat Key, FL 34228

Printed in the United States of America

ISBN: 978-1492229032

Dedicated to all the pets we've known and loved!

When we drove out west, I saw a great big moose.
I asked my mommy, "May I have a moose for a pet?"
She replied, "Goodness, no! A moose is way too big to be
a house pet, but we can get a stuffed moose, and he can
sit on your toy bench."

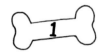
1

At our family picnic, I saw a bunny rabbit race across the field. I asked my mommy, "May I have a bunny for a pet?" She answered, "Goodness, no! A bunny likes freedom to run and hop, but we can get a stuffed bunny, and he can sit on your toy bench."

When we went to the zoo, I saw a very funny monkey swinging in the trees. I asked my mommy, "May I have a monkey for a pet?" She exclaimed, "Goodness, no! A monkey is much too silly to be a house pet, but we can get a stuffed monkey, and he can sit on your toy bench."

7

One day I saw a mouse scamper through the garden. I asked my mommy, "May I have a pet mouse?" She answered, "Goodness, no! A mouse is too scary to be a house pet, but we can get a stuffed mouse, and he can sit on your toy bench."

10

When we went to the circus, I saw a great big elephant.
I asked my mommy, "May I have an elephant for a pet?"
She said, "Goodness, no! An elephant would never fit in
our house, but we can get a stuffed elephant, and he can
sit on your toy bench."

13

When we went to the aquarium, I saw happy, playful dolphins. I asked my mommy, "May I have a pet dolphin?" She said, "Goodness, no! A dolphin has to live in the water, but we can get a stuffed dolphin, and he can sit on your toy bench."

I had lots and lots of furry friends sitting on my toy bench, but I wanted a real live pet to live with me! One day I asked my mommy, "May I have a real live puppy?" She answered, "I think that's a fine idea. The animal shelter has lots of lonely dogs looking for playmates and loving homes." That's where we found Brandywine, and she is my best friend. I made up a song about all my furry friends.

Furry Friends

I love all the animals,
All the animals,
All the animals
In the world!

I love the puppy dog,
And the elephant,
And the bunny rabbit too.

I love the GREAT BIG MOOSE
And the little tiny mouse.
I love all the animals
That live at my house.

I love my furry friends
Sitting on the bench.
I think they look mighty fine.
But the one I love best
Of all the rest
Is my very own Brandywine